Troll Peter Finds a Treasure at the End of the Rainbow

Just imagine! There are people who believe that trolls do not exist. How surprised they would be if they came out on the moor of Jutland and saw Troll Peter and his parents and old Granny sitting by their cooking fire outside Troll Hill. With their pointed ears and tails sticking out behind, anyone could see that they were real trolls. Mind you, unlike most other trolls, they were friendly, good-natured creatures who liked bright and sunny days. So they were up and around all day and at night they went to bed, just as people do. But still, they were trolls.

Now it was summer and the weather had become so hot and dry, that even the trolls longed for some rain to come. The grass withered and clouds of dust rose with every little gust of wind. Troll Peter was very dirty. But he could not have a bath, because the brook had nearly dried out. The troll boy didn't mind. He hated being washed.

But one morning his mother said, "we can't wait any longer for the rain to come. We have to get washed now. Today we'll go to the creek in the meadow and have a good scrub."

"Splendid idea," Granny spluttered. It was not that she liked to be washed, but she thought it would be nice to go for an outing. However, it was a long walk to the creek and it was hard for the old troll woman to drag her feet thought the wild-growing heather. Often she ran out of breath and had to rest, leaning on her knotty stick. But Troll Far and Troll Mor were patient with her. So was Troll Peter. He was in no hurry to have a bath.

Finally they reached the creek and the trolls bathed in the clear, cold water. Of course, the trolls didn't have any soap, so they scrubbed themselves with fine, white sand from the bottom of the creek. But Troll Peter cheated. He just played in the water. Then his mother said, "come on, Peter, let me help you." And she reached down for a big handful of sand.

"No," Troll Peter cried. He sprang out of the water and started running as fast as he could. But his mother followed. In big leaps she chased him over the meadow grass, while Troll Far and Granny stood in the water and roared with laughter.

The troll boy was a fast runner, but he stumbled over a molehill and fell. His mother grabbed him. "Silly boy," she scolded, "running away from his bath like that."

"I – I washed my tail," Troll Peter panted.

"What about your dirty ears?" Troll Mor said and dragged him back to the creek. She scrubbed him until he was pink all over, and the troll boy's screams could be heard far and wide.

After the bath they all sat down to enjoy the bread and porridge, Troll Mor had brought along for lunch. The porridge was just right for Granny's toothless gums, but the bread was dry and hard. She had to dip it into the water to soften it.

Troll Peter was still sulking as he sat eating. His mother tried to cheer him up. "How nice and clean you look," she said and kissed his flushing cheeks.

"I hate bathing," Troll Peter growled. But as his stomach filled up, his mood lifted a bit. Soon he was on his feet, playing about on the soft, green grass.

Granny sat dozing in the sunlight with her feet dangling over the edge of the creek. After a while the troll boy came back and sat down beside her. He took to his ears. They were still burning. "My mother doesn't like me anymore," he grumbled, "or she wouldn't scrub the skin off my face."

"That's not true, Peter," Granny said, hugging him. "You know we all love you."

Troll Peter threw a handful of grass into the flowing water. "All that washing and scrubbing is just a waste of time, Granny," he said. "In a few days I'm dirty again."

The old troll woman patted his cheek. "I know. I agree with you." Then she scratched her tail and chuckled, "but we have a good picnic, don't we?"

Troll Peter's face lit up. "I'm glad you came along, Granny," he said, smiling.

In the meanwhile his parents had been fishing, using their bare hands. So when they started for home, Troll Far carried a sack of fish on his back.

It was late before they reached Troll Hill. At that time Granny was very tired. She sat resting with her hands in her lap while Troll Mor prepared the evening meal. But she certainly had the strength to eat. "A cold bath sharpens the appetite," she muttered, as she stuffed herself with fish and brown bread.

Everybody agreed, and they sat long into the night, roasting fish over the open fire. They ate them hot and crisp and a little bit burned.

The troll family could have spared themselves the trip to the creek. The next day the sky was overcast. "The weather is changing," Granny said. "I can feel it in my tail."

"Yea," Troll Far agreed, looking at the Western sky where some dark clouds had appeared on the horizon. "It seems like a thunderstorm is coming in from the North Sea."

Usually Troll Peter and his parents slept outside on the ground. But now Troll Mor said, "we must prepare ourselves to sleep inside the house tonight." She rose to her feet. "We'd better cut some fresh heather for the beds in there." And then she and Troll Far went off into the moor.

Granny also got busy. She began to carry peat and firewood into the little hut. "If it starts raining, everything will get wet," she mumbled.

During the afternoon black clouds filled the sky and a distant roll of thunder sounded. The air was very calm. Not one leaf moved as the oak tree stretched its branches against the gloomy sky. Fooled by the darkness the black bird flew to the top of the tree and started to sing his evening song. It sounded loud and clear in the still air.

Feeling the tension around him, Troll Peter kept close to his grandmother, who was now preparing turnips for dinner. He was happy when his parents came back home, carrying big bunches of heather on their backs.

"Peter, come and get some fresh heather for your bed," Troll Mor called.

Troll Peter was only glad to have something to do. He spread out the sweet-smelling heather on his bed. Then he went to get the blanket from his outdoor bed under the pine tree. His mother was busy doing the other beds. And now Granny called that the dinner was ready.

As they sat eating by the cooking fire, the thunder grew louder. Troll Far glanced at the sky. "We will soon get a downpour," he said.

"I told you it was a waste of time to go bathing yesterday!" Troll Peter cried.

"I like the rain," Troll Mor said and shuddered, "but not the thunder and lightning."

Troll Peter sat close to his mother. "I don't either. I wonder what makes that awful noise."

Granny leaned forward. "When I was a little girl, my great-grandmother told me that the rumble of thunder is made by a fellow, called Thor," she said. "He is driving on a rock-paved road above the clouds in something called a wagon. It's been pulled by Billy Goats, and he drives so fast that the iron rims of his wheels make sparks. That explains the noise and the lightning."

Troll Mor nodded. "Don't forget the hammer, Granny!"

"Oh, yea," the old troll woman cried, "Thor has a hammer in his hand and once in a while he throws it. Remember, one summer he struck the oak tree."

Troll Mor had been watching the sky. "We'd better go in now," she said. "Come on, Peter."

But Troll Peter was not quite ready to go inside. He sat staring at the black clouds, hoping to spot Thor and his Billy-Goats. Then suddenly a clap of thunder sounded right over his head. He jumped to his feet. "He certainly drives fast," he cried out.

"Hurry up, Peter!" his parents and grandmother called from the door of the hut.

Now a few scattered drops of rain began to fall. Hastily Troll Peter ran to the door. He felt a gust of wind touch his face and he saw the grey haze of rain swallowing the moor. He had just slammed the door behind him, when a bright flash of lightning tore through the air. Then a loud clap of thunder followed.

"It's right over us now," Troll Far said, peering out through the window.

Troll Peter ran to have a look. He pressed his nose flat against the pane of glass and watched the rain come pouring down.

As it grew darker and the rain kept falling the trolls were comfortable inside Troll Hill. Troll Mor had lit a candle, and sitting around the table they ate oatmeal cakes with honey. Troll Peter ate too much and got a stomach-ache. Granny had to give him an extra spoonful of honey to take the pain away. Then it was time to go to bed.

It was still raining heavily, but the thunder had died away. Troll Peter was just about to fall asleep, when a drop of water fell on his nose. Drip! Hastily he pulled the blanket over his head.

Drip-drip! The drops came faster. Drip-drip-drip! Now they began to drip at the foot of his bed. He tossed away his blanket. "It's raining on my bed," he yelled.

Troll Mor sprang out of her bed and grabbed some wooden bowls and placed them here and there to collect the water.

Troll Far rose. "I'll go out to see if I can do something about it." And he strode out into the rain, wearing only his nightshirt.

"I'll help you," Troll Mor cried and went after him, leaving the door open.

"What's going on?" Granny snuffled from her bed.

"It's dripping through the ceiling." Troll Peter told her. "Mor and Far are outside in the rain. I want to go out, too."

Stiffly Granny got out of bed. She sniffed at the fresh air. "Yea, why don't we? If you get wet inside the house, you might as well go outside."

"Where are you?" they called, as they stood in the pouring rain outside the door.

"Up here on top of the hill," Troll Far and Troll Mor called back. "We can't do anything about the dripping. It's too dark and wet."

Troll Peter and Granny began to climb the hillside. The old troll woman had trouble walking as her long, wet nightgown clung to her legs. Troll Peter had to push her from behind. Soon the whole troll family was standing on top of Troll Hill in the dark, rainy night. They stood for a long time, watching the lightning that still flared on the horizon. The rain was falling gently now. Troll Peter lifted his face and let it tickle his nose.

Troll Mor was the first one to break the silence. "I think we should go in and get some sleep," she said and took Granny by the arm to help her down the hill. Inside the hut she found a dry nightshirt for all of them. Troll Peter's bed was soaked because all the bowls had run over. He had to sleep at the foot of his grandmother's bed. At the same time he could warn her feet. They were very cold.

The next morning Troll Peter waded and splashed in the soft, muddy puddles the rain had left on the ground. Everything was green and fresh and the air was good to breathe. Soon the sun came out and the birds began to sing.

The trolls got busy. Troll Far repaired the roof and Troll Mor hung out the blankets to dry. Granny had already been down at the brook. Her grey tail drooped wetly behind her. "There is plenty of water now," she said with a happy look on her face.

Suddenly a beautiful sight appeared. Far out over the moor the sunbeams were playing with raindrops still left in the air. They created a rainbow in a flood of bright colors, red, orange, yellow, blue and green.

The trolls stood with their bare feet in the puddles, enjoying the sight. "Look at that!" Granny exclaimed. "Isn't that beautiful?"

"Yea," Troll Mor said in a soft voice, "the beauty of nature is a gift for all living souls."

Granny wiped her watery eyes. "They say there is a treasure buried at the foot of every rainbow," she remarked.

Troll Peter's eyes grew big. "I'll go and find it," he cried.

"Then you'd better hurry up," Granny cackled, "because when the rainbow goes, the treasure goes, too."

The troll boy did not waste any time. He sprinted over the moor, climbed a hill and scrambled down on the other side. In front of him the rainbow still stood on its pillar of beautiful colors. But Troll Peter had no time to admire the sight. He threw himself down on his knees and began pulling the heather and scraping the soil, which was soft and damp after the rain. It was all green. So were his hands. But right beside him everything was bright red, and a little further away the heather was yellow and blue.

Troll Peter pulled and scraped. Then suddenly he heard a fragile voice. "Don't push me!"

He stopped scraping and stared. There was a small, wild flower standing in a mist of red, changing into yellow. The troll boy thought it was very beautiful. But the most amazing thing was that from the middle of the flower, a tiny face peered up at him. "It's enough that the heather is pushing me, trying to squeeze the life out of me."

Troll Peter gaped. "I – I didn't know that flowers could talk," he stammered.

The small flower bowed its head in modesty. "That's only if we are kissed by a rainbow. But I never thought I should be that lucky. My mother would have been so proud, if she had known."

"Where is your mother?" Troll Peter asked, looking around and scraping at the same time. He had to hurry up before the rainbow vanished.

The flower looked sad. "My mother is long gone like the rest of my family. They were all pushed away by the heather."

For a moment the troll boy stopped digging and stared at the flower with wide-open eyes. "Oh, that's too bad."

Then he noticed that the rainbow was fading, and again he pulled and scraped so the dirt flew all over. He must find that treasure. How deep could it be?

"I'm the only one left now, and soon the heather will choke me, too," the little flower went on. It trembled and Troll Peter saw a drop of moisture run like a tear down its silky petals.

He hesitated. But then he thought of the treasure and started scraping again. Yet, his eyes were drawn to the sad, little plant that was about to be choked by the heather. Suddenly he stopped digging.

"I'll help you," he said. "I'll dig you up and take you home with me to Troll Hill. I'll plant you where you have room to spread out, and one day you'll have a big family again."

The tiny flower smiled happily. It was all yellow now. "That would be nice," it whispered.

Troll Peter had forgotten all about the treasure now. "You are going to live close to a brook," he explained, "and if the weather gets too dry, I'll water you every day."

But he got no answer. The rainbow had gone. The flower did not have a face anymore, and no red and yellow colors. Now it was just a little, blue violet. But the sun shone on it, and Troll Peter thought it was as beautiful as before.

"Let's go home," he said. Carefully he dug up the flower, keeping some dirt around the roots. With both hands he lifted it up and carried it home to Troll Hill.

His parents and Granny sat on the old log, waiting for him. "Did you find the treasure?" Granny blurted out as soon as she saw him.

"No," Troll Peter said, "but I found a little flower."

His grandmother touched the petals of the violet with her old, gnarled fingers. "It's very pretty," she said.

"I thought we could plant it down at the brook," Troll Peter went on. "It will grow and spread out. Then we will have a flower garden."

Troll Mor smiled. "That's what I always wanted." she said, and gently she took the tiny plant into her hand.

Troll Peter eyes lit up. "Then I found a treasure at the end of the rainbow after all," he cried proudly.

"You certainly did," his mother said. "Let's go down to the brook and find a good place to plant the little flower."

0-0-0-0-0-0-0-0-0-0-0-0

Troll Peter's Nightly Visitor

Troll Peter liked his bed under the big pine tree. Filled with heather and straw it was nice and warm. He also had a friend nearby, a spider who lived between the branches over his bed. His name was Jonas. Every night at bedtime they had a nice and quiet talk, just the two of them. But one night the troll boy got a visitor and that changed everything.

As he lay asleep, he was suddenly awakened by a rustling sound. He raised his head, listening. What could that be? Quickly he tossed off his sheep-skin blanket, and with his good troll eyes he made out a mouse bustling about in the straw at the foot of his bed.

"A mouse!" he shouted. "I thought I smelled something. What are you doing here?"

The mouse jerked. "Oh, excuse me," it squeaked, trembling all over. "This is an emergency. I must find a safe place in a hurry."

"Not here," Troll Peter cried angrily, whipping his tail in the straw. "This is my bed. Go away!"

He didn't like mice. His mother didn't like them either. She always complained that they nibbled at her bread. But Troll Peter didn't mind until one day, when he found mouse droppings in the bowl of soup he was eating. Since then he couldn't stand the smell of mice.

"You wouldn't be so nasty, if you knew what happened to me." The mouse began to cry loudly. "I just lost my husband."

For a moment Troll Peter forgot his anger. "How terrible!"

"We had a nice home beneath the root of a tree," the mouse wailed. "Then a fox came and dug it all up and ate my beloved husband. I ran out the back door to save my life and here I am, all alone in the world." Sniffing, she wiped her eyes with her forepaws.

The troll boy felt uncomfortable. "That's a shame," he said, "but you can't stay here." Just the thought of a mouse in his bed gave him the creeps.

"Why not?" the mouse squeaked with a pleading look in her black eyes.

"Because….because we have an owl living in the nearby oak tree," Troll Peter said, hoping that would scare the mouse away. "He'll eat you."

"But he won't know that I'm living in your bed," the mouse told him.

"No, you are not!" Troll Peter yelled, his big ears turning red. "I don't want you here."

But the mouse didn't seem to listen. She was already making herself home in a corner of the bed. Troll Peter felt like grabbing the skin of her neck and throwing her out. But of course, you can't do that to a widow with no place to go.

"Well," he said when he had calmed down a bit, "you can stay here for the rest of the night, but you must leave early in the morning." He didn't want Jonas to find out that he had a smelly mouse in his bed. That would be embarrassing. "And be quiet now. I need my sleep." Then he turned his back to the mouse and slept.

Later on he suddenly awoke. What was that? He heard faint, squeaking sounds coming from the foot of his bed. He lifted the blanket and stared. He couldn't believe his own eyes. The widow had three tiny, newborn mice at her side. "Oh, no!" he burst out.

"Good morning," the mouse said in a hushed voice. "Did you ever see more beautiful babies?"

If Troll Peter had seen them anywhere else, he might have found the baby mice cute, but not here in his own bed. "They are ugly!" he yelled. "They are very, very ugly." Then he added angrily, "you didn't tell me you were going to have a family!"

"I told you it was an emergency, that I needed a home right away, didn't I?" the mouse squeaked.

The troll boy looked at the small creatures drinking milk from their mother. He ground his teeth, knowing that these tiny babies could not be moved for the time being. That meant he was stuck with a whole mice family.

"Listen to me, you old widow," he growled, "you'd better take good care of your stinky brats, or the owl will come and swallow them all in one mouthful."

"Don't worry," the mouse assured him, "I'll make sure they stay under the blanket all the time."

"And keep them away from my toes," Troll Peter went on. "I don't want to have anything to do with any of you."

"That suits me well," Mother Mouse said, smiling. "I like privacy myself."

The noise had woken up the spider. He climbed down his web. "What's going on down there?" he cried, his eyes shining with curiosity. "Did I hear some baby mice crying?"

Hastily Troll Peter dropped the blanket to hide the mice family. But then he realized that Jonas would find out sooner or later anyway. "A mouse came and asked for shelter during the night," he explained. "A fox had just ruined her home and eaten her husband. She had no place to go."

"So you took her in," Jonas interrupted, "and now you have adopted the whole family. You sure have a big heart, Peter."

"I didn't plan to do it," Troll Peter admitted. "She told me she was all alone in the world, but that was not for long. Now my bed is full of mice."

Jonas tried to comfort him. "But you have a lot of room in your bed, Peter."

"Yea, but wait until my mother finds out." Troll Peter said. "She hates mice."

"I know you should not have any secrets for your mother, Peter" the spider remarked, "but in this case I think it's best not to tell her."

Troll Peter nodded. "I guess you're right, Jonas."

A few days later at breakfast Troll Mor said, "I think I'll do my laundry today. In this warm weather the blankets dry quickly, so they can go back on the beds tonight."

Troll Peter stopped chewing and stared at his mother. He thought of the mice. They were still in his bed. "Mine is not dirty," he said.

"Dirty or not," his mother said, "your blanket has to be washed once a year." She was a very clean troll woman.

Now, what was he going to do? But all of a sudden it struck Troll Peter that this way he could get rid of the mice. When his mother removed the blanket, she would see them and throw them out of his bed, and the owl would come gliding and - - oh, no! He could not let that happen! As much as he wanted the mice out of sight, he did not wish them any harm. The babies were still small and helpless. They had to be protected and right now he was the only one who could do it. He had no choice. He had to take care of them until tonight, when the blanket was back on his bed.

Troll Far scraped his porridge bowl. "Then I'll take Peter fishing today," he said.

Troll Peter's heart jumped. There was nothing in the world he wanted more than go fishing with his father, but today he had to stay home and look after the mice. "I - I can't go," he stammered.

His parents and grandmother stared at him. Troll Far raised his eyebrows. "What! You can't go. Why?"

"I - I'm not feeling well," Troll Peter mumbled. That was no lie. He felt awful about the whole thing.

"Oh, darling!" his mother cried.

"Of course, you can go fishing, Peter," Granny broke in. "In a little while you'll feel better."

But Troll Far looked worried. "He really must be sick, if he can't go fishing. Then it's better for him to stay home and rest." Slowly he rose to his feet, grabbed a sack and tucked it under his arm. "I'll see you later," he called as he strode down the path, holding his tail high.

Troll Mor felt her son's forehead. "You are a little damp, but not really hot. Don't run too far out on the moor today. Just stay around here!"

"I will," Troll Peter said meekly.

"Good," his mother said, gently pulling his big ears. "I'll go and get the blankets."

"I'll help you." Troll Peter said hastily. "I'll bring my own blanket down to the brook."

Troll Mor looked surprised. Her son had never been eager to help around the house. She turned to Granny. "Something is wrong with Peter. He is acting strange."

"Oh, well," Granny cackled. "He just wants to be helpful."

Troll Mor still had a puzzled look on her face as she went to the brook to do her washing. "He must be ill," she mumbled to herself.

Granny stroke Troll Peter's cheek with her old, dry hand. "Peter, you little fool, why didn't you go with your father? You love to go fishing."

"I do, Granny, but – "

"Don't you think," his grandmother said, "that I could take care of whatever you are hiding under your blanket?"

Troll Peter stared at her. "How do you know?"

Granny chuckled. "A troll woman does not lose her sense of smell when she grows old. In fact, age just sharpens the senses. I think it's wise of you to keep that blanket of yours away from your mother's nose. It smells strongly of mice."

"That's what I'm trying to do," Troll Peter said with a little smile. Suddenly he felt much better. He didn't mind that his grandmother knew his secret. She might even be able to help him. "Granny, could I hide the mice in the straw of your bed?" he asked, "just for a little while until I find a safe place to put them."

Granny's wrinkled face broke into a grin. "Why not?" She even helped her grandson to carry the mice family inside Troll Hill. "They are cute, so soft and delicate," she muttered as she spread an old blanket over them.

Troll Peter didn't say anything. He knew that Granny thought the mice were his pets. They certainly were not. He didn't like them at all. Yet, he was glad that they were safe in Granny's bed inside Troll Hill.

Down at the brook Troll Peter hastily put his sheep-skin blanket into the water and stepped on it to keep it down. Soon the water had made it so heavy, that his mother had to help him wash it. Then they hung it on some low bushes to dry.

"How are you feeling, Peter?" Troll Mor asked, wiping her hands in her skirt.

"I'm fine now," Troll Peter assured her. All the time he was thinking of the mice. He had to find a safe place to put them. What about the peat stack? The owl would never be able to find them there. So he went over and plucked out a few peat at the bottom of the stack. Then he made a nest of dried grass. That would make a good, permanent home for Mother Mouse and her babies. He would move them out there right away and then forget all about them. Troll Peter smiled. It would be nice to have the bed all to himself again.

Lifting the old blanket from Granny's bed, he said to the mice. "I'll move you to another place now."

"But why?" Mother Mouse squeaked. "We are comfortable here."

"Yea," the babies whimpered, "we are comfortable here."

"You can't stay in Granny's bed any longer," Troll Peter explained. "My mother might smell you. I have made a nest for you in the peat stack."

"When are we going back to your bed?" Mother Mouse asked anxiously.

"When are we going back?" the youngsters echoed. "We like your bed."

"Don't you think it's time you got a place of your own?" Troll Peter replied.

Mother Mouse got a suspicious look in her eyes. "You are not going to leave us in the peat stack forever, are you?"

"We like your bed," the youngsters whimpered.

The troll boy felt uncertain. This was harder that he had thought. Now Mother Mouse began to cry. "Promise you'll come and get us, when your blanket is dry," she sniffed. "We can't do without your bed. It's our home."

"It's our home," the baby mice squeaked at the top of their voices.

"I don't promise anything," Troll Peter snapped.

"Then you might as well feed us to the owl," Mother Mouse sobbed. Tears were splashing down her cheeks, wetting her whiskers.

The small ones also wept. "Feed us to the owl!"

Troll Peter could not stand all that crying. He gave up. "All right," he said, "I promise to take you back into my bed tonight."

Instantly Mother Mouse stopped crying. "I thought you would," she said, smiling through tears and wiping her eyes with her tiny paws.

"We thought you would," the babies cried and bounced about in the straw of Granny's bed.

Troll Peter couldn't help smiling. "Silly mice," he muttered as he gathered them all in his hands. The small ones nibbled his palms and he thought that he would have liked them, if they just had chosen another place to live.

"Remember to come and get us tonight when your blanket is back on your bed," Mother Mouse squeaked, as Troll Peter let them into the nest under the peat stack.

At dusk Troll Far came home with a sack full of shiny fish. Troll Mor lit the fire and sliced bread for supper. Soon it smelled of frying fish all over. Troll Peter's mouth began to water. Also Granny smacked her lips.

"How is Peter?" Troll Far asked.

"He is fine," Troll Mor said and handed her son a big cup of sheep milk.

Troll Peter certainly was feeling fine. At the meal he stuffed himself, gulping down fish, brown bread and sheep milk.

He felt good at bedtime, when he sat under his clean blanket, chatting with Jonas. He was in no hurry to bring the mice back. But then Jonas said, "where are the mice? Did they move out?"

Troll Peter shrugged his shoulders. "They are under the peat stack. I – I think I promised to bring them back here."

"Then you'd better go and get them," the spider said. "It's awful quiet without them."

Troll Peter had never thought of that. He listened. "You are right, Jonas. It is a kind of quiet, isn't it?"

He sprang out of bed and ran to the peat stack, "It's just me," he whispered. "I'm coming to get you." Nobody answered. He plucked out some peat. "Where are you?" he whispered again. But the peat stack was as quiet as before.

All of a sudden Troll Peter felt guilty that he had waited so long to get the mice back into his bed. He called again and he removed more peat. He tore most of the peat stack apart, but he found no trace of the mice family. Now he really began to worry. Could the owl have found them after all?

He ran to the oak tree. The old owl was just about to leave for his nightly hunting trip. Troll Peter swallowed twice, trying to get rid of a lump in his throat. "Hello Owl," he said in a husky voice, "I wonder if you have seen some mice around here lately."

"Yea, now that you mention it," the owl said in his deep-down voice, "I just had some for supper."

The troll boy jumped. "You did! What did they look like?"

"They were furry and had tails, and they tasted very good." The owl rolled his eyes upward. "It was a most delicious meal."

Troll Peter turned on his heels. He felt awful. "I have something to tell you, Jonas," he said gravely, when he reached his bed. "It's about the mice."

But he had barely spoken the words, when he heard a happy squeaking and four, small creatures jumped into his lap.

"There you are," Mother Mouse cried. "We have been looking for you."

Troll Peter could hardly talk. "I – I went to get you," he stammered. "But you must have left the peat stack before I came."

"Did you have something to tell me, Peter?" Jonas asked curiously.

"Not anymore." Troll Peter slid down under the blanket. He drew a deep breath of relief. He never thought that he could be so happy to see the mice again?

But he was not the only happy one. Mother Mouse was humming as she tidied up her corner of the bed. And the youngsters played and squeaked with joy. They nibbled Troll Peter's nose, pulled his straw-colored hair and climbed his big ears. But he knew it was not to tease him. It was because they liked him so much. And suddenly he realized that he had come to like the mice too. He even liked their smell.

When Mother Mouse had finished her house-cleaning, she stroked her whiskers to tidy herself. Then she wiped her children's faces with her red, little tongue and got them to bed. Soon they were fast asleep, curled up in their nest.

Troll Peter lifted the blanket and looked at them. "They are very cute," he said in a tender voice.

Mother Mouse smiled and a joyful tear ran down her cheek. "Then you don't think they are ugly anymore?" she whispered.

"No," Troll Peter said with a grin on his face. "They are not ugly. They never were." And with a finger he very gently stroked one of the youngster's furry back. It was as soft as a feather to touch.

0-0-0-0-0-0-0-0-0-0-0-0

Uncle Bridge Troll Comes for Dinner

There was a rumor going among the birds of the moor. It said that the Bridge Troll was going to visit his relatives at Troll Hill one of these days. Troll Far heard two sparrows talk about it, but he didn't know whether to believe it or not. So he went straight to the old owl. That was the only bird he trusted.

"It's true - true," the owl hooted, rolling his eyes. "Your cousin, Thorwald, will be coming for dinner the day after tomorrow."

The trolls were pleased. They had not seen the Bridge Troll for years. So they decided to have a feast to make him feel welcome. Troll Far and Troll Mor hurried to the creek to catch some fish to be smoked by the cooking fire. Also Granny got busy. She dug up a lot of earthworms and made them into a pickled dish.

"Do you want to taste, Peter?" she offered, wiping her hands on her apron.

But the troll boy wrinkled his nose. "Worms are food for the birds," he said.

His grandmother swung her grey tail cheerfully. "Your uncle likes them. Just wait and see."

Troll Peter danced about on the grass. He had never seen his uncle. "I can't wait to meet him."

The next morning Troll Far said, "I'll go hunting for some feathered game. I know that Thorwald will be hungry when he comes tomorrow night. He has a great appetite."

"Can I go with you?" Troll Peter eagerly asked.

"No," his father replied, "you don't have the patience to lie still in the heather, waiting for the wild ducks to come close enough for me to grab."

When evening came Troll Peter went up to sit on top of Troll Hill, waiting for his father to come back home. The sun had just disappeared in the West, leaving a golden glow on the sky. Before long he spotted Troll Far out on the moor with a sack on his back. He ran to meet him.

"Nobody will go hungry to bed tomorrow night," his father said, showing him the birds, he had caught.

That night the troll boy watched as his mother and grandmother stood by the flickering fire, plucking the ducks. They threw away the bigger feathers but saved the down for pillows. They also kept the tip of the wings. They made good dusters.

Later on, when he lay in his bed under the pine tree he told Jonas about his uncle's visit. "He is coming tomorrow night for dinner," he said to the spider.

Jonas sprang from his web, trailing a thread. "Gee, I didn't know you had an uncle."

"I do," the troll boy said. "He lives under a bridge in South Jutland, and he is coming all the way up here to visit us."

"How interesting!" the spider cried. He was swaying back and forth in the soft breeze. "You must tell me all about it when you come to bed tomorrow night."

"I sure will," Troll Peter promised.

After the spider had said goodnight the troll boy listened to his parent's and Grandmother's conversation as they sat relaxed by the fire. "That cousin of mine has always been adventurous," Troll Far bragged, "and he is brave, too."

"Yea," Troll Mor said and shivered. "He must be fearless since he dares to live under a bridge where people travel all the time."

Granny leaned forward. Her eyes glinted in the dark. "In a way it must be exciting to be a Bridge Troll. There is always something going on."

"Well, I wouldn't like it," Troll Far said, scratching his tail. "I like the quiet life out here on the moor where people never come."

"Me, too," Troll Peter mumbled from his bed.

The next morning Troll Mor swept the flat stone outside the door. "I have to make flour so I can bake some bread," she said.

"I'll help you!" Granny cried. She ran into the hut and came back with her apron filled with grains of rye. With her hands she sprinkled them on the doorstep. Then Troll Mor sat down on her knees to grind the grains into flour, using a small, flat rock.

In the meantime Troll Far had lit a peat fire in the oven that was built in beside the fireplace. And when it had burned out he scraped the ashes into the bottom of the chimney. That left a hot oven for Troll Mor's baking. She was already making the dough. Soon it smelled of freshly baked bread all over Troll Hill.

All day the trolls were busy. Troll Far went to the bog to catch frogs to be fried over the fire. Troll Mor picked nettles for a salad and Granny swept the ground. Troll Peter also got chores. He had to collect pine cones to be put on the cooking fire at dinnertime to give the smoke a festive smell.

As the sun went down the troll family sat outside Troll Hill, waiting for their guest to arrive. To look their best they had been at the brook to wash their hands and faces, and Troll Far and Troll Mor had put on their best clothes. Old Granny had even turned her apron around, because it might be a bit cleaner on the other side. As for Troll Peter, his ears were still dirty, but who would notice that in the dark?

The meal was ready, too. On a spit over the fire three wild ducks were roasting. They were nearly done. The rest of the food was placed on the ground beside the old logs that served as seats for the trolls. There were plates with fried frogs, smoked fish, snail pies and honey-glazed grasshoppers. Then there were bowls filled with pickled worms and nettle salad. Of course, the newly-baked bread was there as well together with a jar of honey. And beside it all stood a bucket of water to wash the food down with.

Troll Peter had never seen so much food before. His mouth watered. "I wish my uncle would soon be here," he said impatiently.

The trolls were not the only ones looking forward to see the Bridge Troll. That night the owl did not fly out at dusk as usual. He stayed home on his branch in the oak tree, staring out over the moor to be the first one to spot the guest. The other birds also sat waiting although it was far past their bedtime. They had spent all day preening their feathers to look pretty. Too bad it was already getting dark.

The time dragged. Everybody sat very still. The only sounds were the humming of the mosquitoes and the sizzle of juice from the roasting fowls, dripping onto the glowing firewood.

"What a beautiful evening," Troll Mor said, breaking the silence, "so nice and calm. No wind at all."

But that was not quite true. Of course, the wind was there. Troll Peter could feel it breathe on his neck. The wind was just quietly waiting, like everybody else.

"What if he does not come after all?" the troll boy said anxiously.

"Sure he will come," his father said, smacking a mosquito on his arm. "You have to remember that your uncle does not like the daylight as we do. He might have slept all day somewhere in the shade."

Just then they heard a rumble. At the same time the owl hooted twice. That was a signal that he had seen something. In the next moment the Bridge Troll came rushing out of the dark in a cloud of dust.

Troll Mor, Troll Far and Granny sprang to their feet to greet him. But Troll Peter hid behind his mother's skirt. There he stood peeking out, looking at his uncle. He was a very big troll with long, hairy arms and crooked legs. And his long tail was flung over one of his broad shoulders.

"Gee," Troll Peter muttered. "What a tail!" Yet, he didn't really like the sight of his Uncle. His eyes sat close together under black, bushy eyebrows. He also had tufts of dark hair sticking out from his beaked, warty nose – and was he ever dirty all over.

"Hi there!" the Bridge Troll called in a blustery voice. "How are you doing up here on the moor?" Then he saw all the food and his eyes twinkled. He also spotted Troll Peter behind his mother's skirt. "Don't be shy," he bellowed and with his dirty fingers he pinched Troll Peter's cheek, leaving a red, swollen spot.

"Ouch!" Troll Peter howled, whipping his tail in the dust. "You hurt me!"

The Bridge Troll roared with laughter, showing big, yellow teeth. "He has a nice temper, that little son of yours, ha, ha!"

He squeezed Troll Far's out-stretched hand and hugged Troll Mor and Granny so hard it nearly took their breath away.

"It's good to see you again, Thorwald," Granny cackled, "and you have not changed a bit."

"You too, Aunt Pernilla." And the old troll woman got another hug.

"Please sit down," Troll Mor said, seating him on the log as far away from her son as possible. "Dinner is ready!"

But as she lifted the over-cooked birds from the fire, they fell apart and landed on the glowing firewood, sending out a shower of sparks.

Troll Mor, Troll Far and Troll Peter cried out in dismay. But the Bridge Troll laughed so hard that he had to hold his stomach. Granny was not concerned either. "That just makes the meat more tasty," she giggled. And with a poker and a sooty stick she helped Troll Mor to pick up the pieces.

Uncle Bridge Troll snatched some of the meat from the ashes. He stuffed it into his mouth and grinned. "I've never tasted anything better," he cried.

Soon they all sat on the logs, ready for the big meal. "Help yourself," Troll Mor said with a smile.

Thorwald didn't need to be told twice. With one hand he grabbed a handful of fried frogs, and with the other hand he took a smoked trout and a piece of duck. When he had eaten that, he slurped up a bowl of pickled worms. He shoveled food into his mouth so fast that he nearly choked. Fat and juice from the meat dripped into his beard and down onto his clothes. Then he scratched his hair with greasy fingers and reached out for more food.

Troll Peter sat staring. He nearly forgot to eat. He saw the food disappear into his uncle's big mouth, and he saw his chest move with every mouthful he swallowed. Also Troll Far, Troll Mor and Granny helped themselves. They seem to realize that if they wanted some of the food, they'd better hurry up to eat.

The birds, sitting in the nearby trees, craned their necks not to miss anything. They were impressed. What a meal!

When the worst hunger had gone, the trolls began to talk. "How is the traffic over your bridge nowadays?" Troll Far asked.

"There is a little bit of everything." Thorwald said as he swallowed a big piece of snail pie. "It's mostly people traveling on foot. But there are also a few horse-riders and once in a while a wagon."

As Troll Peter sat chewing, he noticed that his uncle's chest moved again, this time in circles. It looked very strange. The troll boy got alarmed! He suddenly realized that there must be something alive, wriggling about inside that shirt. What could that be? A snake? A rat? Or something else? He looked at his parents and Granny. But they didn't seem to have noticed anything unusual.

"Then there are those cattle drives," the Bridge Troll went on. "They are horrible."

Granny looked up from her food. "Cattle drives? What's that?"

"People are silly creatures," Thorwald explained with his mouth full. "They feed cattle on the meadows up North, and then they drive them all the way down to Germany to be sold for something called money."

"Money?" Troll Far said. "What is that?"

"I don't know. I've never seen any, just heard of it." The Bridge Troll scratched his neck. "But people seem to like it."

"They do have strange habits, don't they?" Granny remarked as she munched on a honey-glazed grasshopper.

"Back to my story," Thorwald went on, "I'll tell you, when a herd of roaring and tramping cattle crosses the bridge, everything inside our home rattles and dirt falls down from the ceiling."

Troll Mor shook her head. "How awful!" She rose and put a few more pine cones on the fire. "How awful!"

"The worst thing is that they always come in the daytime, when we're trying to sleep," the Bridge Troll said.

Troll Mor didn't like to talk about those horrible creatures, called people, especially not with her little son around. That might give him nightmares. She changed the subject. "How are Trolline and the children?" she asked.

"They are fine. The boys are thriving," the proud father boasted. "They are not that old, but they are already little monsters, doing all kind of pranks."

"You were advanced for your age too, when you were a child," Granny said with a chuckle.

"Those boys make so much noise that travelers sometimes are afraid to cross the bridge." Thorwald grinned. "They think that a hideous troll is living under it."

"Yea, but that's true," Troll Peter blurted out.

"Listen to Peter," roared his uncle, laughing so loud that a sleepy bird dropped down from a branch. "He certainly has a good sense of humor." And with his long arm he reached over to give the troll boy another friendly pinch.

Quickly Troll Mor put a bowl of salad into his hand, and Granny handed him a couple of fish. "Do eat, Thorwald," the old troll woman croaked, "or we may think you are sick."

But the Bridge Troll was not sick. Greedily he ate the salad and the rest of the fish. He emptied the last bowl of pickled worms and even drank the juice. He also ate the rest of the bread, and he stuck a dirty forefinger down into the honey jar and licked it. Then with a burp he rose to his feet.

"An excellent meal," he grunted, wiping his hands on his sheep-skin vest. "I'm so stuffed I can't sit down any more." And standing up he munched on a handful of honey-glazed grasshoppers, which was now the only food left. Then he lifted the bucket of water, put it to his mouth and drank in big swallows.

"That's right, Thorwald," Troll Far said. "Just help yourself. There is plenty of water in the brook."

"Thank you, but I'm full now," the Bridge Troll sighed and clapped his own belly. Then suddenly a shriek sounded from underneath his shirt. Troll Peter jerked and sprang over to his mother. His parents and Granny also looked alarmed.

"Oh, I nearly forgot," Thorwald cried. He unbuttoned his shirt, reached inside and pulled out a little, furry animal with a round face and a tail.

Troll Peter stared. So that was the one, who had been moving about. But what kind of creature was it? "This little kitten ran after me, when I passed a farm," Uncle Bridge Troll told. He handed it to the troll boy. "I thought that Peter would like to have it."

Troll Peter took the kitten into his arms, and the little cat rubbed its head against his chest. He thought it was the cutest thing he had ever seen.

"From now on you won't have any mice around Troll Hill," his uncle roared.

"That will be nice," Troll Mor said.

"Does - does it eat mice?" Troll Peter stammered. Without his mother knowing it, he had four pet mice in his bed.

"You'd better believe it," Uncle Thorwald bellowed. "All cats like the taste of mice."

Troll Peter handed the kitten back. "I don't want it."

"Peter, what are you doing?" his mother said. "Sure you want it. Say thank you to your uncle."

"I don't want it," Troll Peter repeated and stamped his foot.

Granny was the only one who knew about his pet mice. Now she broke in. "If Peter doesn't want a cat, he shouldn't have one," she cackled.

The Bridge Troll looked bewildered. Then he grinned. "No hard feelings," he said. "I'll just take it back. I pass the same farm on my way home anyway."

"We'd better give the little creature something to drink," Troll Mor said. She hurried over to milk the sheep that stood nearby. The little kitten was very thirsty and quickly licked up the milk.

Then the Bridge Troll put the cat back under his shirt. "I'd better be going now," he said and flung his long tail over his shoulder. "I have a long way home."

"Won't you stay until tomorrow night?" Troll Far suggested. "Then we could talk some more."

"Not this time," his cousin replied. "I can't leave Trolline and the boys alone for too long. We're expecting a new baby to arrive any time."

Troll Mor clapped her hands together. "That's good news," she said.

"That's for sure," Granny agreed.

Then the Bridge Troll pinched both of Troll Peter's cheeks, shouted good-by and strode off, disappearing into the summer night.

Troll Far and Troll Mor stood side by side, watching him go. They were happy that the dinner party had gone so well. Granny also looked happy. But Troll Peter rubbed his cheeks. "Ouch, it hurts!" he whimpered.

"Darling," his mother said, hugging him. "It will soon go away."

"I'll see to that," Granny cried. She ran into Troll Hill and found a new jar of honey under her bed. She dipped a spoon deep into the syrup. "This will take the pain away," she said.

Troll Peter licked the spoon until there was no trace of honey left on it. Then he smiled. In spite of his burning cheeks, he was proud to have an uncle like that. "He sure ate a lot," he said.

Granny chuckled. "Yea, your uncle has a fine appetite, and I told you that he likes pickled worms, didn't I?"

0-0-0-0-0-0-0-0-0-0-0-0

Troll Peter Sees People

"I have thought of something," Troll Far said one night when the troll family sat around the crackling fire outside Troll Hill. "We have never had a vacation. Why don't we take a trip?"

Granny, Troll Mor and Troll Peter looked very surprised. A trip!

Troll Far put some more twigs on the fire and twitched his long, hairy tail away from the flying sparks. "I always wanted to show Peter the highway, where people travel," he said. "That would be a good experience for him."

The little troll boy sprang to his feet, shouting with joy. The road where people traveled! He remembered he once had asked his grandmother what human beings looked like. She had told him that they look ugly with small ears and no tail at all. He had shivered. Yet, he thought it would be exciting to see those creatures.

"Splendid!" Granny cried. "Then we may see some travelers." She was very old, but she still liked adventures.

But Troll Mor didn't think it was a good idea. She was afraid of those monsters, called people. She certainly did not want to go near them. She'd better find a good excuse in a hurry. "It would be too long a walk for Granny," she said.

"Me?" the old troll woman cackled. "Not at all! I would enjoy it!"

"What about Peter then?" Troll Mor went on. "He is only a small child with short legs."

"Don't worry," Troll Far said. "Peter has strong legs. And I'll carry Granny some of the way. They'll make it. Just wait and see."

Troll Mor sighed. She was not happy about it. But she had to admit that it was a good time of year to go traveling, because if they ran out of food they could eat the berries of the moor.

Now everybody got busy preparing for the trip. Troll Peter went down to the brook to water the little violet his mother had planted, so it wouldn't dry out while they were gone. He also went to his bed to explain to his pet mice that he had to take his blanket with him. Therefore they had to move into the peat stack, while he was away. "Be careful and look out for the owl," he said. "He is the one who looks after Troll Hill while we are gone."

He also told Jonas about the vacation. "It sounds like fun," the spider said with a dreamy look in his eyes. "You must tell me all about it, when you come home again."

Already the next morning the trolls set out, wandering over the moor. Troll Far carried all the bedclothes on his back and Troll Mor had a big bundle of food under her arm. Behind them came old Granny, dragging her feet and supporting herself with a knotty stick. Last of all came Troll Peter, carrying two skin bottles filled with water. They all looked happy and free.

They traveled all day among the hills of the moor, resting very often. When evening came, they stopped at some low bushes. Troll Far threw his bundle down on the heather. "We'll stay overnight here and have a good sleep," he said. "It has been a long day for Granny and Peter."

"First we must eat," Troll Mor said, unpacking her sack. She held the bread against her chest while slicing it with her knife. Then she spread a bit of honey on each slice. Troll Peter was hungry. He ate a lot.

After the meal he played about on the heather until his mother called, "Peter, it's bedtime." She had spread out a couple of sheep-skin blankets with the wool side up. The other ones she used for covers. That made a nice bed. Yet, the trolls kept all their clothes on when they lay down. That was the easy way to do it.

Troll Peter looked at the stars high overhead on the dark sky. He felt warm and safe, lying close to his father. He thought of the spider and his pet mice who had to stay home at Troll Hill while he, Troll Peter the lucky one, went on a vacation.

The next morning the trolls were early on their feet. Soon they were out on the open moor. Here the West Wind was the master. It greeted the trolls by jerking and pulling their hair and clothes. They walked slowly. Granny had trouble dragging her feet through the heather. But then Troll Far took his old mother into his strong arms and carried her. They all wore homemade skin boots, because all that walking would have been too hard on their bare feet. After another day of traveling, Troll Peter got impatient. "When will we be there?" he asked. "I can't wait to see the road. What does it looks like?"

"I'll tell you the story of the road," Troll Far said as they sat resting in the evening. "You see, it's very old. Even my grandfather didn't know when it came into being. Most likely it was only a footpath through the moorland for a very long time. Then came the tracks of wheels, and now it was called a road."

"How big is it?" Troll Peter held out his arms.

"I can't tell you," Troll Far answered, "but it's a long stretch. I know there are places along the road, called inns, where people can eat and rest."

"Then there must be many travelers," Granny broke in.

"As far as I know, it's the only big road in Jutland," Troll Far went on. "It is very wide because when the tracks get too deep or muddy, people just make new tracks beside the old ones. That way the path trodden long ago has ended up being a big, wide highway. And that's the one I want to show you."

"I can't wait," Troll Peter repeated and danced about on the heather.

Troll Mor shuddered. "Just the thought of people moving about on the moor gives me the creeps," she said.

"They sure are hideous creatures," Granny agreed.

Troll Far scratched his beard. "As long as they keep to the road, we have nothing to fear," he said. "It's far away from Troll Hill."

After a good night's sleep the trolls went on for another long day of traveling. It had started to darken when they reached some brushwood. Now Troll Far dropped the bedclothes on the heather. "This is where we are going to stay," he said. "We can hide in the bushes and overlook the road at the same time. Tomorrow morning we'll go over and show Peter all the tracks."

Troll Mor looked worried. "What if some people come by?"

"Then we'll hurry up and hide." Troll Far said with a glint in his eyes. "You know how often I sneak about at people's places when we need something. I just make sure they don't see me."

"I wish we had some more food," Troll Mor complained. "We don't have very much left - and no water at all. I had hoped we were going to stay close to a stream."

"Don't worry about food," Troll Far answered. "I'll see to that. Just lie down and go to sleep. I'll be gone for a while." Then he grabbed the skin bottles and strode off, holding his tail high in the air.

Bewildered Troll Mor, Granny and Troll Peter stared after him as he disappeared in the dusk. Troll Mor was the first one to speak. "Let's find some berries to eat before it gets too dark," she said.

Soon Troll Peter found a spot where cranberries sat red and ripe on low, creeping plants between the heather tufts. "Over here," he called.

"Not so loud, Peter," his mother hissed.

When they had eaten enough berries to soothe the worst hunger, they made their beds in shelter of the bushes. Then they sat in the growing darkness waiting for Troll Far to come back. Granny and Troll Peter got drowsy and lay down. The old troll woman snored right away. But Troll Peter was sure that he could not sleep until his father was back. But all of a sudden he heard voices. He opened his eyes. It was daylight and he heard the larks warble high over his head. And then he saw his parents and grandmother sitting nearby, eating. The night had gone and his father was back.

"Good morning, Peter," his mother called in a low voice. "Come and get your breakfast." She sounded happy.

Troll Peter rolled out of bed. He rubbed his eyes. He could hardly believe what he saw. Three whole loaves of bread and a big, smoked haunch of sheep lay on the heather. The skin bottles were also filled up with water. His grandmother looked fresh and full of life, as she sat chewing on a piece of mutton. "What a breakfast," she muttered.

Troll Mor handed her son a thick slice of bread and meat. He grabbed it and started eating. He figured that there must be one of those inns nearby, since his father had been able to get all this food. The thought was scary, but the food was good and he was hungry. He gobbled down the bread and meat and reached out for more.

When they had finished eating, the trolls hid the food and the blankets in between the bushes. Now they were ready to go over to the road. As they walked, they turned their heads from side to side to look around. But nobody was there.

Soon they stood on the old highway, a rough, sunken road. On both sides there were a lot of other sandy tracks. Some of them were fresh, but others were faint and overgrown by heather and coarse grass. In the early morning-light the road seemed lonely and deserted.

For a long time the trolls said nothing. They just stood very still, thrilled to be standing where people could appear at any moment. Naturally Troll Far kept an eye on the road in both directions. Granny stood smiling, leaning on her knotty stick. Her grey hair flowed in the wind. But Troll Mor was nervous. She shuffled her feet, eager to go back and hide in the bushes. Troll Peter thought it was very exciting. He stood looking down at the tracks that people had made with their wheels.

Suddenly he spotted something lying on the ground. It was a little, round, flat thing that glittered in the sun. In fact, it was a silver coin but the trolls didn't know that.

Troll Peter picked it up. "What is that?" he asked his father.

"I don't know, but it must have belonged to some people," Troll Far said, looking closely at it. "They might have thrown it away, or perhaps dropped it by accident."

"Can I keep it?" Troll Peter asked eagerly. He liked the feel of the coin, so smooth in his hand. He would like to take it home to play with.

"No," his mother said sharply. "Look! It has human marks on it. It could burn a hole in your pocket. Hurry up and throw it away!"

"Let's see how far you can throw it," Granny snickered.

Troll Peter looked at her and smiled. He took several running steps, and then he threw the silver coin far out into the heather.

"Good boy," Troll Far said.

"I think we should go back and hide," Troll Mor said anxiously. She took Granny by the arm, gently pulling her away from the road. But Granny was not ready to leave.

"Wait, wait a bit!" she croaked.

But Troll Far said, "yea, it's time to go back to the bushes and wait there."

They hid in the brushwood for a long time, waiting for something to happen. But everything was quiet. Only the wind sang its own tune, as it swept over the sandy tracks.

Suddenly Troll Far whispered, "I hear something."

Troll Mor, Troll Peter and Granny held their breath and listened. They heard nothing but the rushing of the wind. But after a little while they all heard a faint rumble, and then the creaking sound of wheels. Soon they saw a wagon, pulled by two oxen coming along the road. When it came closer they could make out a person, sitting on a board that was put across the top of the wagon.

"There you have a human being, Peter," whispered Troll Far.

Troll Peter hid behind his mother's skirt, peeking out. He was pale and his knees were shaking as he stared at the hunched-up creature in the wagon. With his own eyes he now saw one of those mysterious beasts, called a man. He was wearing a big, wide-brimmed hat so it was hard to see his face. But the trolls heard him yell and crack a whip. His voice sounded hoarse and grumpy.

"So that's the way the tracks are made," Troll Peter thought, as he saw the wheels working their way through the heather.

"Isn't he ugly?" Granny whispered. Troll Mor nodded silently.

The wagon was not quite out of sight before Troll Far perked up his ears again. "I can hear something else now," he muttered, "but I can't figure out what it can be."

Soon they all heard a steady, rumbling sound in the distance. It became louder and louder. "The road is bewitched," Troll Mor cried out. "Let us run!" But Troll Far held her back. Troll Peter was also frightened, and even Granny had a scared look on her face.

Suddenly Troll Far began to laugh softly. "Now I know," he said. "Remember that my cousin, the Bridge Troll, told us about large herds of cattle being driven along this road. That's what it is."

The rumbling grew stronger and soon a large group of animals appeared far out on the road in a haze of dust. When they came closer, Troll Peter saw that they had big, rounded horns sticking out from their foreheads. They looked big and wild, and they seemed to be everywhere. He covered his ears. What a noise! The air vibrated from the sound of roaring and tramping cattle. As they passed, the smell of the warm and dusty animals drifted into Troll Peter's nose and made him sick. He turned and threw up.

"Oh, no!" his mother cried. "I knew he was too young to see things like that."

Troll Far hissed at her. "Look!"

Some men had appeared. They were the drovers with sticks in their hands. They shouted and chased the cattle. Troll Peter stared in disbelief. Were these really the same creatures as the one, who sat in the wagon? They had arms and legs and they walked the same way as trolls. He craned his neck to get a better look, but by doing that his straw-colored hair stuck out from the bushes. One of the animals, a young steer, thought it was a tuft of hay and came galloping over. Some more cattle got curious and followed. Now they all crowded around the bushes where the trolls were hiding. The troll family ducked low into the brushwood not to be discovered by the men.

"What's going on over there?" one of the drovers shouted. And he ran over, yelling and swinging his stick. But the cattle did not move. Sniffing and tripping over one another, they stood with their heads in the bushes. They seem to wonder what the trolls were doing in there.

Another drover rushed over and with his stick he chased the steer that had started the whole thing. Frightened, the animal sprang into the air and pushed to the other ones. Then they all began pushing each other toward the road. And soon they were on the move again.

The men passed close to the troll's hiding place. If Troll Peter had stretched out his hand, he could have touched them. He was so afraid, that he could hardly breathe.

"How stupid of the cattle to stop like that," one of the drovers said. "I can't wait to get to the inn. I'm very thirsty."

"Yea," agreed the other one, "my throat is so dry I can't even spit."

The trolls sat very still until the cattle and the drovers had disappeared. "Ugh," Troll Mor groaned, "was I ever scared?"

"Me, too," Troll Peter said. He was still pale, but he felt better now.

"I have to admit it was a close call," Troll Far remarked. "But I think that if those people had seen us, they would have been more scared than we were."

"They wouldn't have believed their own eyes, would they?" Granny remarked with a toothless grin on her face.

"No," Troll Far said, "I don't think they have ever seen a troll close-up. We always make sure of that."

For a long time they could hear the sound of the animals and see the cloud of dust far out over the road. "I didn't know there were so many big animals in the world," Troll Mor said.

"Where are they going?" Troll Peter wanted to know.

"Don't you remember that your uncle, the Bridge Troll, told us about herds of cattle being fed on the meadows up North and driven down to Germany to be traded for something, called money?"

"Money, what's that?" Troll Peter asked.

"I can't tell you, because I don't know," Troll Far said. "Your uncle didn't know either."

"It must be some kind of food," Troll Peter concluded.

"That reminds me, I'm hungry," Granny cackled in her dry voice.

"Yea," Troll Mor said, "let's get some food and a drink of water to rinse the dust out of our throats."

"We certainly need it," Troll Far agreed. "But we've had a good day. We have seen what we came for. Tomorrow morning we'll start on our trip home."

All of a sudden Troll Peter longed for Troll Hill. He thought of his friend, the spider, and his pet mice. He became so cheerful by the thought of going home, that he threw himself on the ground, rolled in the dust and shouted with joy.

"Look at the little darling," his mother said. "He is homesick!"

And the next day they began the long journey home over the moor.

0-0-0-0-0-0-0-0-0-0-0

CPSIA information can be obtained
at www.ICGtesting.com
Printed in the USA
LVIC040928010812
292449LV00006B